If I Can, You Can.

Sam Wages Johnson

Copyright © 2025

All Rights Reserved

If I Can, You Can.

Dedication

Dedicated to my parents:

Rick & Tommie Ann Johnson

Thank you for your love and support.

Sam Wages Johnson

Acknowledgment

Special thanks to:

Chris Glinski, LPC, CMAC, NCC &

Bill Eubanks, CAC

These two men helped change my life forever.

About the Author

Sam Wages Johnson was born and raised in Lawrenceville, Georgia, where he grew up in his family's funeral business. He spent ten years addicted to opiates, heroin, and painkillers, and lost more than twenty-five friends to overdose. When fentanyl began taking lives around him, Sam often worked the very funerals of people he had used with days before. Standing with their families and seeing their grief left a mark he could not ignore.

Even as his addiction worsened, an abscess from dirty needles nearly cost him his arm, and an overdose in a friend's car still didn't stop him; those faces stayed with him. When his family drew a hard line, Sam knew it was time. On October 4, 2015, he decided he would change his life or die trying.

This book is his way of giving back, using what was meant to destroy him to help anyone who sees their story in his. We're on the same road to recovery; some are just a little farther along.

If he can, you can.

Table of Contents

Introduction:

Who I Am

Growing up at my family's funeral home, I had seen a lot. I always thought that would be part of the reason I became a drug addict. To my surprise, that wasn't the case at all. Looking back, seeing my family help people in our community get through the worst times of their lives was actually inspiring—especially when you look at the level of care they provided. And I feel it's common to think that way if you grew up like I did.

What's not common, however, is working the funerals of 20-plus friends who overdosed and lost their lives to addiction. I would get high with my friends on Tuesday and be working their funeral by Saturday. Addiction destroyed so many of my friends' families, and I was right there to witness it all. Looking into the eyes of my friends' parents and family members, telling them how sorry I was for their loss—all while high out of my mind. The best way I can describe that period of my life is The Twilight Zone.

I consider myself tough—always have. But what I saw would bring even the toughest man to his knees. I saw the pain in their eyes. I could feel the gaping wound in their soul, a wound that will never be filled no matter what they do. That's the reality of addiction. And that was soon enough going to be the reality for me and my family—if I didn't make the decision to change my life forever.

This is my purpose. *This* is my calling. As much as I try to run away from my past, it will never leave me. No family deserves to go through that kind of pain, and as long as I'm above ground, I will do my part.

I wrote this book based on what I would have liked to know before and during treatment. Hindsight is 20/20, and this book was created to give you the best chance at stepping up, changing your habits, and making sure—as a man or a woman—that your family will never have to go through that pain.

Simply put…

If I Can, You Can.

Chapter 1:
The OD

Therefore, I say to you, whatever things you ask when you pray, believe that you receive them and you will have them.

-Mark 11:24

I knew I shouldn't have gone out there that night. I had this sinking feeling in the pit of my stomach that something bad was going to happen. Contrary to popular belief, addicts still have a conscience—and the ability to know what's right and what's wrong.

On the way out to the Southside of Atlanta, we got a flat tire. Standing on the side of GA 400, I remember looking up at the sky. I could hear God telling me not to go. I could have run away. I could have yelled at one of my best friends, who was driving, and told him this was wrong—that we were ruining our lives. I could have called my parents and asked them to come get me, to help me turn my life around. I could have done so many things to not go that night. But there were no conversations like that going on in my head. There was just silence. A dead silence—of a man who had thrown his entire life away and was about to experience what so many friends from his hometown already had.

No addict ever thinks they're going to overdose— unless they intentionally want to. I always thought I was too smart, too tough, too smooth to let that happen. I never really wanted to die, but I remember toward the end of my addiction thinking, "Well, if I do happen to die, it won't be the worst thing." That's how deeply entrenched I was in self-pity. Gone were the dreams and goals I once had as a happy child. And here I was, facing my reality on the side of the road.

Without missing a beat, I got back in the car, and off we went. The ride down there was always bad, because I was always detoxing—feeling like I wanted to die. The ride back was always one of eerie silence. That feeling of getting away with something you know you shouldn't be doing—but somehow, it gave you a strange sense of peace and comfort.

We pulled up to a dark, old, run-down convenience store. No gas pumps. Not a soul in sight. Just a boarded-up building that hadn't seen a customer in years. My friend got out of the driver's seat, went behind the store, and came back about five minutes later. It was already late, so we didn't have time to pull over and shoot up. He was driving, and as a team, we worked together to load up the syringes. While he drove, he tried desperately to find a vein in his arm—but couldn't. So he leaned over and handed me the needle.

"DON'T DO ALL OF THIS, SAM," I remember him saying in his deep baritone voice.

Now, my buddy was—and still is—a beast of a man. He stands 6'3", weighs 285 pounds, and is solid as a rock. Not a softie by any means. One of those guys that if he loves you, he loves you—but if he doesn't like you, you better watch out. Definitely the kind of man you want in your foxhole.

Me, in the passenger seat, trying to prove myself, I took the syringe from his hand. I found a vein, and without hesitation, I shot the entire dose into my arm. Every time I used, I would count down from ten. I usually got to seven or six before it hit me. I remember getting to maybe eight—and then, silence.

He lifted my eyelids and saw my eyes had rolled back into my head. What I didn't know was that once I started to overdose, he put a strip of Suboxone in my mouth. When he did, I bit down—subconsciously—with all of my strength, clamping onto his fingers. He started to panic, struggling to get free, until finally, he was able to pull his hand away.

The next thing I remember was looking down at the car we were in. It looked like someone had cut the roof off, and I was hovering above it, watching us from the top of the gas station. It was like an out-of-body experience—and then suddenly, it was like someone snapped their fingers, and I woke up.

When I came to, the first thing I saw was him shaking me violently.

"SAM... SAM... SAM, YOU'RE ALIVE!!!" he was screaming at the top of his lungs. I had never heard that tone in his voice before—panic, raw and desperate. And when I heard it, I knew it was serious.

I kept wanting to go back to sleep, but he wouldn't stop shaking me. He kept at it until I finally told him to stop, but he wouldn't.

"You just f*cking overdosed, Sam! Oh my God, I

thought you were dead!!!" he kept yelling, over and over.

Once he saw that I was really awake, he took off and drove us back to our side of town. The entire ride back, I was in a daze. I just felt… sad. I knew I was about to become another name—another person from my hometown who lost their life to addiction. I couldn't believe it had finally happened to me.

And honestly? A part of me was upset when I woke up.

The crazy part is, after that night—I didn't stop.

When he dropped me off at my car, I remember staring up at the sky. I stood there for a good five minutes, trying to figure out how my life had gotten to this point.

The worst part was, I had no idea how it got so bad.

Like me, my friend got lucky enough to finally turn his life around, and today, he is a successful businessman. He and his wife have recently celebrated the birth of their first daughter.

If I Can, You Can.

Chapter 2:
Why Did I Start?

Unforgiveness is like drinking poison and waiting for the other person to die.

-Marianne Williamson

I wish this was a simple answer, but it's not. It's very complex. We all have a pair of glasses that we see the world through, and my lenses were cracked, to say the least. Every word we say and every action we take are based on our beliefs—and there are no exceptions to this rule. For the longest time, I believed I was a failure. I believed everyone was out to hurt me. I believed God was cruel and enjoyed seeing me in pain.

Just like all of us, when I was a child, I went through some things. But unlike many people, I chose to keep it all to myself. I never understood the value of expressing my emotions. I never knew that, as a man, I was allowed to cry. I thought I had to soldier up—24 hours a day, 7 days a week. I had no concept of forgiving people. I didn't know that failing at something and believing you are a failure were two totally separate things.

I felt alone. I felt no one loved me. I felt lost. I felt nothing good was ever going to happen. I felt abandoned by God. I felt like no one cared. I felt sorry for myself.

I came from a nice home. Two parents. Church.

Sports growing up. Lots of friends. But none of that really mattered, because I still felt alone. Your thoughts control your feelings, and your feelings control your actions. I thought I had nowhere to go. I thought I had no one to turn to. I thought I was a loser.

If you looked differently than me, I judged you. If you went to a different church than me, I judged you. If you were raised differently than me, I would sit high up on the hill and look down at you, judging you. The whole time I sat there judging people for being different, the only person I was really judging was myself. I was so insecure as a man that the only way I felt good about myself was by putting other people down.

I had built up these emotional walls to protect myself. And the thing is, at first, it worked. The walls I built kept out hurt and pain. When I thought about people and relationships, I immediately associated them with pain. But those same walls that kept away hurt and pain also kept out happiness and joy. It was a protection mechanism—but not a very good one.

It took me a long time to recognize that sometimes, pain is just a part of life. And that's okay. I didn't know it was okay to hurt. I didn't know that sometimes, that's just life.

I have a saying: "People are going to people." What I mean by that is—you can't control people, and you can't control the way the world works. I have to take the good with the bad. As human beings, we were made for relationships. That's why, when people get arrested, they get put in jail—

away from their relationships. And when you mess up in jail, they put you in isolation.

My ego caused me to take everything so personally, and it nearly cost me my life.

This life can be tough.

But this life is worth living.

If I Can, You Can.

Chapter 3:
Addiction Doesn't Care

Your thoughts control your feelings. Your feelings control your actions. Your actions determine your life.

-Bob Proctor

People care. Some people care what your religion is. Some people care what the color of your skin is. Some people care what your sexuality is.

Addiction does not.

Addiction couldn't give a damn about any of those things. It will seek and destroy a Christian family just as quickly and ruthlessly as it will a Muslim family. You think addiction cares what color your skin is? You think addiction cares how much money you have in your bank account?

Think again.

In treatment, I met people from all walks of life. We didn't share the same background, or the same religion, or even the same likes and dislikes. We didn't have any of those usual bonds. But what we did share was hurt—and pain. We were all in the same boat, whether we liked it or not. And for the first time in my life, I started to care about other people—regardless of what they looked like or where they came from.

Whether you're waiting on the pawn shop to open with your stolen goods in tow, or you're waiting on a bank to open its doors so you can withdraw $1,000 to go get high, addiction is non-judgmental. It could care less what you look like or who you pray to at night.

All it knows is that once it has its hands wrapped around your neck, it will slowly but surely squeeze the life out of you—one bag of dope at a time.

Sound depressing?

It should.

And that was my life—for almost a decade.

The reason I wrote this book is because over that decade, I saw families absolutely destroyed—beyond repair. And by the grace of God, I came so close… but I made it out.

Survivor's remorse is real.

I always thought to myself, "Why did you make it out, Sam?"

How come so many people you ran around with are no longer with us, but you're still here?

That question ate me up for a long time—until I figured out the only logical conclusion:

I was spared so I could turn around and help people not make the same mistakes I did.

In short:

I turned my pain into my purpose.

If I Can, You Can.

Chapter 4:
The Most Selfish

If you think the price of winning is too high, wait until you get handed the bill from regret.

-Tim Grover

You have to be there for you.

Some people were mandated to treatment by the courts. Some were "fam-dated" to treatment—sent there by their families. A few of those people made it. But the majority didn't. That's just the reality of the situation.

You can use your family as motivation at first—but in the end, this has to be all about you. When you make the decision to live the right way and do the right things, healthy relationships become the byproducts of you handling your business.

Trust me.

The selfishness I had was twofold. My addiction was selfish to the core—causing pain to myself and to the ones who cared about me most. Every day I woke up, the first and only thing I could think about was getting more dope.

Who could I rob?

Who could I steal from?

Am I going to jail today?

Those were my daily problems. I didn't care about being there for my family or friends. If I had to show up somewhere, you could bet your bottom dollar I was only going if I had enough drugs to get me through it. It got so bad that people started to think something was seriously wrong with me—because I was always "sick." I always had an excuse. I missed out on so much with my family and friends because my number one priority was getting high.

It was all about Sam.

And I didn't give a damn about you.

That's the life of an addict.

Ironically, my recovery would take the same level of selfishness—but now with a different intention. I guess in a sense, when I first wake up, it's still all about Sam. But now, it's about Sam so I can prepare myself to give to my family and friends.

That's the kind of selfishness it takes to turn your life around.

It's like what they say on airplanes—they don't tell you to put the mask on your child first. They tell you to put the mask on yourself.

Once the mask is on you, then you've got the time and ability to help others put theirs on.

You never want to go back to the old you.

Why would you?

Think about it. The old you is what got you into treatment in the first place. The old you is what led you to this very moment.

After I left treatment, I talked with a good friend of mine from high school. He said, "Man, you sound like the old Sam."

"Nah, bro," I replied. "This is the new Sam."

My life had been broken into pieces. Now it was my duty to take those broken pieces and rebuild myself.

One day at a time.

But more importantly—five minutes at a time.

Addicts are resourceful people, as we all know.

Addiction was once my curse.

Now, addiction was going to be my gift.

If I Can, You Can.

Chapter 5:
Game Over

Circumstance does not make the man; it reveals him to himself.

-James Allen

In October of 2015, I had been on opiates in some form or fashion for eight years. I didn't know how to live my life without them. They gave me energy. They gave me a friend. And they gave me more pain and discomfort than I could have ever imagined. By that point, I had already been to jail, overdosed, almost had my arm amputated from an abscess—and on top of that, I had buried 20 of my friends who had lost their lives to addiction. Like a lot of addicts, I was frail, weak, and hopeless.

I still couldn't see myself getting clean. I couldn't even fathom it. Just like any addict, I had my little schemes: breaking and entering, pawn shops galore, and stealing anything and everything I could from anyone around me. I didn't care about myself—so you really think I cared about you? Not a chance.

But at this point, all of my games were up. I had no one left to rob or steal from. It had been a couple of days since anything had been in my system, and I was starting to detox—badly. I found solace on the bathroom floor. When I got hot, I'd roll over onto the cold tile. When I got cold, I'd roll over onto the bathroom rug. I remember hearing footsteps on the stairs, and before I knew it, my father was standing over me. He looked me dead in the eyes and said, "What happened to you, Sam? You used to be big, strong, going places. What happened?" I remember those words verbatim like it was yesterday. The crazy thing was—I still didn't have an answer.

My bedroom at my parents' house became my tomb. My pillow and mattress had turned into my deathbed. I was going to die. No doubt about it. But it was different this time. By the grace of God, my family and friends finally found the strength and courage to turn their backs on me. That is true love. My addiction had held my family hostage for so long, and now they were done with me. I sat there and thought to myself: people lose their families every day. But I'll be damned if I lose mine to drugs.

At that point, I heard a voice whisper in my ear: "You can do it, Sam. It won't be easy—and it shouldn't be—but you can do it." It was at that very moment that I made the decision—I was either going to change my life or die trying. There is so much power in making a decision and standing by it, come hell or high water.

My father reached out to a family friend who sent over a list of treatment centers. I knew I had a long-term addiction, so I needed long-term treatment. As much as I hated the idea, I knew it was what I needed. Everyone is different in how much treatment they need, but without a doubt—I needed the longest one I could find. I was ready. I was either ready to die or to change. And I didn't want to die. For the first time in my life, I made the decision to man up. This was my new reality.

So I detoxed alone in my childhood bedroom for eight days before I went into treatment—and I will never forget it. I will never forget the pain and hurt my body went through. I'll also never forget the Wahlburgers marathon that was on TV night after night, or the Geico commercial with the song "The Final Countdown." Those lasting memories stay with me as a reminder of reaping what I had sown.

If I Can, You Can.

Chapter 6:
Prepping For Rehab

Your present or past results have absolutely nothing to do with what's going to happen from this point forward.

-Ray Stanford

As the days crept closer to treatment, a whole new wave of emotions hit me. I wasn't just detoxing physically and mentally anymore—I was starting to realize I might have just volunteered to go to the nut house for a year. Will they put me in a straight jacket? Will the rooms be padded? Am I not going to have my phone? Will anyone even visit me? Will I complete the program only to run right back into my old habits?

I remember lying on my bed, sick as a dog. I couldn't believe my life had spiraled to the point where—for lack of a better term—I was a junkie. I've never really liked that word, but sometimes it just is what it is. So many emotions were running through my head in those final days before treatment. My mind was racing—and who could blame me? I had gone from nearly a decade of daily drug use to detoxing on my own to preparing for rehab for an entire year. But again, these were all real problems I had brought on myself. No one forced dope into my veins. No one told me to become a criminal. I did that. This was me, finally taking full responsibility for my actions.

The wildest part of it all? There was only one common denominator in every single one of my problems: me. It was crazy what I thought was important at the time. My biggest concern wasn't survival or healing—it was whether or not I was going to have my phone in treatment. Imagine that. I'm at death's door, my family has washed their hands of me, and I'm worried about Instagram. I had a serious case of FOMO. My manhood was oozing insecurity. It was all so symbolic of where my priorities were.

I also couldn't stop thinking about what people would say when they found out I was in rehab. That had become my MO: fake and inauthentic, while obsessing over what others thought of me. I knew people were finally going to see through the facade I'd built. My glass house was about to shatter. But again, I came to realize—none of that mattered. I'd rather people know I'm in rehab than have them standing over my casket saying, "Man, Sam had potential." The truth hurts.

Mom and Dad couldn't save me anymore—nor should they. They tried their best, God bless them. But this was something that had to be done for me, by me. Lying there on my "death bed," I made the decision to turn my life around. And this? This was where the rubber meets the road.

There is so much power in making a decision.

I had a goal: go to rehab and turn my life around, no matter the cost.

If I Can, You Can.

Chapter 7:
Do I Even Deserve This?

If you work hard on your job you'll make a living. If you work hard on yourself you can make a fortune.

-Jim Rohn

Guilt and shame are such powerful emotions. I did terrible things all in the name of drugs. One thing I noticed was that once I was out of treatment, everyone had pretty much forgiven me for the bad things I had done. The hardest part was forgiving myself. Guilt and shame had built up in my mind and soul, and at first, it was tough to believe I even deserved to change.

No one can play the role of victim like an addict. And when I'd sit around getting high all day, most of the thoughts running through my head were just replays of all the mistakes I had made. I used to apologize until I was blue in the face—"I'm so sorry," "I swear to God I'm never going to do it again." I talked such a good game, but my actions proved those apologies were hollow. I didn't mean them. As I always remind myself: the best apology is changed behavior.

The more I thought about all this, the more I realized I could not let my family go through the same pain I had watched so many other families suffer when their loved ones overdosed. That kind of wound in the soul never truly heals—you just learn to work around it to carry on through life. Seeing friend after friend lying lifeless in their caskets—many times at my family's funeral home—hit me hard. Addiction has real-life consequences. Watching family after family of people I grew up with endure that pain is something I still can't shake. And the worst part? All that pain and suffering might have been avoidable if they had just gotten the help they needed.

All I could think about were the good times—the fun I used to have with my boys, chasing girls, laughing so hard my mouth would hurt. I missed that. I missed waking up without having to run to my "special little place" in my room to poison myself just to get the day started. I had ENOUGH. This is my life? This? This BS? This is what I wake up for every day? Just to screw over everyone I come into contact with—only because I don't want to look inward and do the work?

That's not life. I deserve to be happy just as much as the next man. That little voice in my head reminded me: I deserve all the good things in life. Now—right now—is my time. Not six months from now. Not after I go get high "one last time." This is my shot to go out there and make it happen.

Siri, play *Lose Yourself* by Eminem.

If I Can, You Can.

Fitness is a great way to keep your mind busy and feel better. From 153lbs almost having my arm amputated to where I am today. Don't sit and read this and say miracles don't happen.

One of my mugshots. This was one of those nights where me and my buddy (who saved me from my OD) shouldn't have made it out alive. He's the only person I used with who I still talk to. Our friendship has stood the test of time.

Me in my addiction. Just a lost & hurt kid.

To think I almost lost my family because of my own addiction is heartbreaking. Now we're much happier.

Got into acting after rehab. This is me (white shirt bottom left) on set of a nationally televised commercial.

With my parents two weeks into treatment at our fundraiser. Notice the scabs on my face. I remember feeling so lost at this event. So glad I did not leave treatment and finished!

The tally marks represent all of my friends who lost their lives to addiction. With that I have my favorite Bible verse 2Timothy 1:7.

Chapter 8:
You're Exactly Where You Need To Be

Your mind is like soil. You can plant a seed of sweet corn and a sixteenth of an inch away you can plant nightshade, a deadly poison. One will grow in complete abundance as the other. Your mind doesn't care what you plant, but you must plant something.

-Earl Nightingale

As I was told in treatment: your best thinking got you to this point. The way you know how to live life—your problem-solving skills, your decisions, your actions—led you exactly to where you are now. Hearing that was a hard pill to swallow, especially as a man. To look in the mirror and admit that I didn't know what to do? That was tough. On top of that, my life was on the line. My addiction had gotten so bad that I was willing to do whatever my counselors told me to do. I thought I was so big and tough, but deep down, I was just a hurt kid who didn't know how to deal with the pain.

The Billion Dollar Question: Why do some people experience trauma and turn to addiction, while others go through trauma and never touch a drink or a drug in their life? I used to think those questions were important for me to answer—but they're not. All I can say now is, God bless those people. Hopefully, they'll write a book someday, because I sure don't have the answer to that question—and neither do you.

What did matter was that I was finally open to finding a new way to live. Once you get around other people who struggle like you do, you start to see firsthand that it is 100% possible to turn things around.

It was hard to ask for help. I kept thinking: how can I admit to my family that I need help when I can't even admit it to myself? That's the mind game of denial—and it's real. But denial is also the first wall that has to come down.

My ego was a big part of the reason I destroyed my life. I kept banging my head against the same wall, hoping for a different outcome—or hoping someone would come save me. You might have people's concern or sympathy, but everyone, including your spouse and your parents, has their own life to live. The only way this process works is if you, in effect, give up. Not give up on life—but give up your narrow views, your broken ways of doing things.

Results don't lie. And if you're sitting in treatment— or even just thinking about it—you're probably in the same boat I was in. The crime isn't that you got addicted to drugs or alcohol. The crime is knowing you have a problem, and still making the conscious decision to stay stuck—to not get help—and to keep hurting the people who love you... including yourself.

If I Can, You Can.

Chapter 9:
Your New Home

For God did not give us a spirit of fear, but of power, love and self-control.

-2 Timothy 1:7

The first morning I "woke up" at rehab was the moment it really set in for me. I say "woke up" in quotations because, of course, I didn't really sleep. Still detoxing after eight days will do that to you. No phone, no cigarettes, no laying around on the couch trying to figure out how to scam my way to $100 for the day. I remember lying in bed after maybe two hours of sleep and taking a deep breath. That breath was filled with as much anxiety as it was relief—relief that I was off the streets.

But now came the question: How do I go about rehab? The answer came to me through an intern who had just completed the program. That morning, he asked me to take a ride with him to Home Depot. And yes—I thought about jumping out of the car going 45 mph and hoping this would all just be a dream once I hit the concrete. But then he started explaining something to me in a way I could immediately identify with.

He asked if I'd ever moved into a new house. I nodded. Then he said,

"Remember when you moved in and you didn't

know where anything was?

You have to figure out where all the door handles are, where the windows are in case you need to open them.

You have to figure out where the bedposts are—so in the middle of the night, when you have to get up and go to the bathroom, you won't stub your toe. But at first, you don't know, so you will stub your toe a few times.

Eventually, though, you figure it out, and it becomes familiar."

My first reaction? Man, not me. This is not my home! I don't live in rehab.

There goes my ego again—immediately putting me back in denial.

The reality was: this was my home. Not forever, but for right now, this was home.

And when I kept the goal in mind—"I will turn my life around or die trying"—I could breathe again. I reminded myself this whole process of being in rehab wasn't my end; it was my beginning.

The beginning of building the strongest, toughest, kindest, and most trustworthy man I could possibly become.

If I Can, You Can.

Chapter 10:
Mr. Fix it

Old emotional scars cannot be doctored or medicated.
They must be "cut out", given up entirely, eradicated.

-Maxwell Maltz

I had gotten so used to that cloudy feeling over my brain. Thinking clearly was something I had forgotten I could even do. For almost ten years, I wasn't really living in reality.

People would go about their business, living happy and healthy lives—and there I was, stuck in my own little world. Every decision, from the moment I got out of bed to the moment I went to sleep, revolved around how I could further my addiction. Half the time I was awake, I was living in fear of the next day, trying to figure out whether I could find more dope or if I'd have to be sick the entire day. Talk about wear and tear on your mind and spirit—I was fully detached from society and from life.

Once I was in treatment and the drugs were finally out of my system, I was able to truly think clearly for the first time in a long time. And guess what happened?

I panicked.

As long as I was high, it was easy to take my mind off the chaos I had caused in my life and in my family's lives.

But once you're sober and clear-minded, all of that negative energy you put out into the world starts to come back. The only difference now was that I felt it—instead of being numb to it.

The first instinct is to "run out and fix it." I didn't like feeling the consequences of my actions, and I was still trying to hold onto that last bit of "control" I thought I had. I saw so many people leave treatment within the first week or so, just because they had finally realized the amount of damage they had caused to their loved ones.

But consequences are there to teach us lessons. It's God's way of letting us know we can't just run around doing whatever we feel like doing and expect everyone to be okay with it.

There was a guy I went to treatment with, and once he detoxed, the full weight of what he had done to his family hit him like a ton of bricks. He legitimately ran away. His reality finally caught up to him, and his instinct was to go back out there and try to control the situation. He wanted to skip the process—to go from A straight to Z. But that's not how this works. That's not how real and lasting change happens.

There's that ego again.

One of the biggest reasons I changed my life was because I finally saw the effect my addiction had on my family. The pain I caused them—not by accident, not by chance, but through my actions—is what drove me to say: enough is enough.

A decade later, I don't think I would've made it if I hadn't had to sit there in treatment and feel the pain I caused my loved ones.

I had to let go of control and face the full effects of my addiction—on myself, and on them.

And always remember this: the best apology is changed behavior.

If I Can, You Can.

Chapter 11:
Five Minutes At A Time

Environment is more important than heredity.

-Karl Menninger

A million miles a minute.

That's how I would've described my mind when I first got to treatment. It was the fear of the unknown. Safe to say, I was on high alert.

One of the first pieces of advice I got was, "Take it one day at a time."

That felt like too much. I didn't know if I had one full day in me. Just the thought of what I might have to go through—or that I was going to have to talk about my past—scared me beyond belief.

But there was something to that advice. I just had to break it down even further.

I remember walking around campus, picking up trash, and repeating to myself, "Five minutes at a time. Five minutes at a time."

That was more my speed.

The truth is, you have to tell yourself whatever you need to in order to get over that first hump in treatment. There's a period when you're just getting your feet wet—

and a part of you still wants to leave. What you're doing is so foreign to what you're used to. But that's a good thing. You're stepping into a whole new world—and yeah, that can be intimidating.

I had a habit of taking something small and turning it into World War III in my mind. It was hard for me to stay present at first. The fear of the unknown was eating away at me.

Looking back, it's kind of funny—I was being so dramatic. But I ended up finding real comfort in the advice I got from people who had been in treatment long before I got there.

Remaining present in the moment is how you change your future.

The problem was, I was so used to thinking about the past that the present didn't even cross my mind. But when you stay in the present, you give yourself a chance to breathe—and to make the next right decision, the one that can positively shape your future.

For the first time in a long time, I was being honest with myself. I understood this wasn't going to be a quick fix—nor should it be. Even to this day, I work on myself constantly. And when I feel overwhelmed, I still say to myself, "Five minutes at a time."

Because now I know—if it worked then, it'll work now.

That's the beauty of finishing treatment: if I could do that, then whatever is currently bothering me doesn't stand a chance.

I built myself from the ground up—and I did it all five minutes at a time.

If I Can, You Can.

Chapter 12:
Two Immediate Changes

Do whatever you have to do to resist temptation.

-Tupac

I always thought that no one had it worse than me. It felt like no one understood my pain—and on top of that, no one ever cared.

I wasn't interested in sharing my story, nor was I interested in hearing yours. But that changed when I went to treatment.

After just a few days, I started to hear people talk about their pasts. Some of the stories made my skin crawl. I remember thinking how could anyone do that to a child? What kind of monster did they have for a parent?

One of the first things I learned in treatment was that people did have it worse than me.

When you sit in your head as the victim, it's hard to see that. But hearing the horror that some people went through as children made me immediately appreciate my own upbringing.

It also made me feel a little ashamed that, for so long, I thought no one had it harder than I did.

The truth is, no matter what you've been through,

there are people out there right now experiencing ten times the pain and trauma.

The second thing I learned was that I could actually care for someone else. I'm not talking about the surface-level, politically correct form of caring—where you feel bad for someone. I'm talking about a deep connection to someone you barely know, where you actually want to be there for them.

When your addiction is as bad as mine was, the only thing you can think about is yourself. But once I was in a room full of people going through the same struggle I was, I started to feel something different. I started to feel peace—because I realized I wasn't alone.

And when you're in the thick of addiction, it's very easy to forget that.

I began to bond with people—and those bonds were based on pain. We didn't connect because we looked the same or liked the same music.

Remember the chapter about how addiction doesn't care? Well, this was that, in full effect.

I was getting close to people 30 years older than me. I was connecting with people who had never believed in God or been to church a day in their life.

From the outside looking in, we had nothing in common. But from the inside looking out, we were all the same.

And that connection existed solely because the

people who shared their stories had the courage and humility to tear their walls down. They were open to being vulnerable with people they'd only just met.

That takes guts.

And it showed me that I could do the same.

If I Can, You Can.

Chapter 13:
Your Therapist Care, But Only So Much

Depending on what they are, our habits will either make us or break us. We become what we repeatedly do.

-Sean Covey

At first, it was difficult for me to trust the counselors. I had this fear I had conjured up in my head—that after I found the courage and strength to expose my secrets and trauma, they'd make fun of me behind closed doors.

I created this scenario that kept me closed off from everyone. Paranoia would be a good word for it.

I had been made fun of as a child for the way I looked, and I carried that same energy with me into class every day. I saw other people opening up, but I wanted no part of it.

To me, everyone was the enemy. My ego was in overdrive.

After I went through treatment, I stayed on staff for a year to work there—and that's when it finally became crystal clear: These counselors don't take their work home with them.

The last thing I ever wanted to do after a full day was go home and think about what people had shared in class. I didn't want to run and tell my friends or family about the stories people had been brave enough to tell.

It was nothing like I had imagined when I was still in the program.

It finally hit me—after all that worrying and paranoia—I was safe. I was in a safe space where I could, in effect, spill my guts to professionals who respected the fact that I wanted to change.

It was such a sigh of relief. Mentally and emotionally, I could finally breathe.

I had been so tense for so long, always thinking everyone was out to get me. But that was no longer the case.

I wasn't telling my secrets and trauma to friends, to my parents, or to a family friend they thought could "get me off the dope." I was telling them to trained people who understood and who held space for healing.

What I came to realize was this: maybe I was the one who wanted to gossip outside of class—not my counselors.

Treatment can be boring at times. And since I wanted to talk about other people, I projected that energy onto the staff. But it just wasn't true.

There's a sacred trust among the people you're in treatment with. Like they told me: you have to get comfortable being uncomfortable.

There has to be a level of respect and honor—not in a flashy, Las Vegas kind of way—but in the way that says:

What we say in class stays in class.

If I Can, You Can.

Chapter 14:
Honesty

You are the only problem you will ever have and you are the only solution.

-Bob Proctor

Back when I worked at the treatment center, one of my jobs was community outreach.

I would invite other treatment centers to come check out our place—and vice versa.

I also went out into the community to share my testimony. As you can imagine, I met a lot of successful people in the treatment field and got to know many counselors well.

After a while, I started to notice the same patterns. See, a lot of addicts will enter treatment, stir up drama, and try their very best to get kicked out. That way, when they talk to their families, they have plausible deniability.

"I wanted to finish treatment, but they kicked me out over some BS."

That was a popular one I heard often. The truth? They never really wanted to be there in the first place.

And like most people carrying a guilty conscience, they get loud. They'll shout, complain, and bash treatment centers as long as someone's listening.

That's where I believe a lot of treatment centers get a bad rep.

In getting to know other programs, I came to the conclusion that most treatment centers are solid institutions. They're 100% committed to helping and guiding you toward a better version of yourself.

But all of this—every bit of it—boils down to one thing: Honesty.

Whether you realize it or not, you and the treatment center are on the same team. It didn't feel like that for me at first—not even close. But at the end of the day, both sides are working toward the same goal: a better you.

What I learned in treatment is that the program gives you a path. They hand you a kind of map to follow, but it's your job to fill in the blanks.

That map is based on the information you give to your counselors.

There will come a point—and it came for me—when that map either changes your life or it doesn't. And that all depends on whether you're honest...or whether you keep lying like you've been doing for years.

If you lie to them, they'll create a path based on false info—and it'll lead you nowhere. That's not on them. They're working with what you gave them.

I can't tell you how many people I saw leave treatment completely lost—because for months, they'd done nothing but lie. And when it came time for the rubber to meet the road, they had no foundation.

And of course, it was never their fault. It was always someone else's.

At first, I wasn't honest either. Honesty was a foreign language to me.

I wanted to look bigger and badder than I really was. I didn't want to be honest about my family and the struggles we'd carried for generations—all the way back to my grandfathers. I thought it was embarrassing. I didn't want my classmates to know. I told myself I was "protecting them."

But at that point, that was neither here nor there. The past of my family wasn't what mattered anymore.

Why?

Because the future of my family was on the line. My future was on the line.

How could I break the generational curse if I ended up six feet deep from an overdose?

It's not easy to be honest in treatment. You're about to unload your deepest trauma and secrets to a group of strangers.

But this is the part where you find out who really wants to change—and who still thinks they've got "one more run" left in them.

Once I made the decision to change my life, I was

willing to do whatever it took. That meant facing all the anxiety and embarrassment I carried from my past.

And once I did?

It wasn't anxiety and embarrassment anymore. It was relief.

Chapter 15:
If You're Going To Leave, Fine, But Leave Tomorrow

The honest man reaps the good results of his honest thoughts and acts; he also brings upon himself the sufferings that his vices produce.

-James Allen

When I was in treatment, there was an 83-year-old man named Gene who would come in during the weekdays and sit with anyone in orientation or anyone who had just come off the streets. Gene was old school—tough and wise beyond his years—and he had zero filter. He'd turned his life around back in the 1970s and carried a wealth of knowledge. He'd been there himself, so he knew exactly what it was like to be in the position I was in at the time.

If you get to rehab and don't feel like leaving when you first arrive, you're lying to yourself. Being real and honest is the only way you're going to make it to the end.

I saw people stay for a week, a month, even a couple of months. I also saw people leave after just a couple of hours. It's understandable why someone would want to leave treatment. After all, who ever imagined at nine years old that they'd end up in a treatment center? I know I didn't. Anytime someone in the program said they were going to leave, Gene would say, "If you want to leave, fine—but leave tomorrow.

You're already here today, so give it 24 hours. If you still feel like leaving tomorrow, then leave."

Option 1: Cut and run. Keep running from your reality and the consequences of your choices—just like always—hoping your troubles will magically disappear.

Option 2: Take a breath, calm down, and realize that where you are now is way healthier than where you were. More importantly, you're not in treatment forever. You're in it for a small window of time—an opportunity to build the new version of you, the one who can be a productive member of society and show up for the people you love.

Everything started to change for me when I realized I had the ability to sit, listen, and respond—instead of overreacting. That pause between feeling and reacting gave me the confidence that I could finally turn my life around. It allowed me more control over my impulses and prepared me for the next withdrawal pain, the next craving.

On the contrary, overreacting led to bad decisions that only dug my hole deeper, sinking me deeper in the see of self-doubt and in confidence.

Ego is a silent—sometimes not-so-silent—enemy that will keep destroying your life if you let it. But it doesn't have to be that way.

If I Can, You Can.

Chapter 16:
Mental Health Is Proactive Not Reactive

Out of suffering have emerged the strongest souls; the most massive characters are seared with scars.

-Khalil Gibran

For most of my life, I didn't understand mental health. I just sat back, took whatever life threw at me, complained to a few people, and hoped it would go away. Spoiler alert: it never did. I felt suffocated by the daily problems life brings, always reacting emotionally instead of responding intelligently.

Sure, some bad things in life are completely out of our control—but not all of them. When you take charge of how you react, you'd be surprised at what you can stop or fix simply by making time for your mental health.

I'd venture to say that 99% of mental health is just getting ahead of the game instead of letting life keep kicking you while you're down.Journaling For me, journaling, working out, eating right, and reading are the four pillars that keep me in a good headspace—and we'll dig into each of these in the coming chapters.

Back then, my daily routine—when I still believed I was just a victim of my circumstances—looked very different. I'd toss and turn all night, knowing I'd be sick in the morning without drugs. When daylight came, I'd lay in bed for hours, doing nothing but figuring out who I could steal from or rob. Most days, I wouldn't even bother brushing my teeth or taking five minutes to shave. When I finally found the strength to get up, I'd check my track marks, looking for signs of infection or deciding if I needed to ice my veins to keep the swelling down. Then I'd go outside to search for a used cigarette butt. I couldn't afford a pack anymore, so I'd head to local businesses, lift the lid off those long plastic cigarette bins, and grab handfuls of strangers' discarded butts to stash in an old empty pack.

From there, I'd sit in my car with no AC in the hot Georgia sun and start scheming. Of course, I had my dirty syringes and cotton with me. After somehow managing to get drugs, I'd shoot up in my car, pass out for a while, and then head back home. That was every single day. Rinse and repeat.

Now? I take pride in my mental health. Do you know what it feels like to go from that routine to the one I have now? It's hard to describe. It's one of those feelings you can't put a price on. Every single day I wake up, journal, work out, eat right, and read. And every time I do those things, I'm cementing the New Sam—and Old Sam can't stand it.

I know Old Sam is still back there, lurking, trying to stick his nose in my business. But when I knock out those four daily tasks, I take control of my day. I send a signal to my brain that I'm in charge now—not the hurt kid who helped destroy my life. Do I have days where I miss? Not really. That's how important those four things are to me. They're just part of who I am today.

And the reason I've gotten here is simple: my addiction was that bad. My family deserved more. My friends deserved more. And yes—last but not least—I deserved more.

If I Can, You Can.

Chapter 17:
Spirit AKA God

It takes a tough person to make a tender chicken.

-Frank Purdue

What I learned in treatment is that we all have a concept of a higher power—aka God. Even if you don't believe in God, that's your concept of it. For a lot of people, this is a touchy subject—and how could it not be? The way I always looked at it was: if God is real and loves me, then why won't He come rescue me? All-powerful, right? Can move mountains, right? So let me get this straight: He can do all of that, but He won't come do it for me?

Correct. God won't do it for you—because God works to and through you.

I always felt God was cruel. My concept of God? Judge, jury, executioner. In my mind, He wasn't a loving Father—He was the warden of a prison I could never escape from. I felt like God knew exactly what tempted me and exactly where my weaknesses were. He would dangle that carrot in front of me, fully aware I'd grab for it. And when I inevitably did, I imagined Him shaking His head in disappointment, just waiting to hammer down the gavel. I assumed He purposefully put me in situations where I couldn't win, stacking the deck against me so that when I failed—and I always did—He could point and say, "See? I told you so." When I tell you I played the victim, I mean it.

What wasn't easy for me to grasp was the concept of free will—because to me, free will means responsibility. And as an addict, few things gave me more nightmares than taking responsibility. What I failed to recognize was that God was showing me the consequences of my poor decisions. That little voice in my head, the one telling me what's right and wrong—that was God. When I'd wake up detoxing, feeling like death after a day of stealing and using—that was God. Through our decision-making, we create our reality. And for the longest time—whether I knew it or not—I created a living hell for myself here on Earth.

What I was taught is that, when it comes to God, the most important thing is having a real and honest relationship. Just like with any loved one, you're going to have ups and downs. You'll have days when you feel like you're closer to God than anyone, and some days you might question whether God is even real. That is real. That is honest. And that's also probably not what you were taught growing up by your local preacher or your grandparents.

Here's what I didn't realize until later: God isn't afraid of your questions. He's not intimidated by your anger. He's not sitting there with a clipboard, ready to cross your name off the list because you yelled at Him or doubted Him. If anything, that honesty is what makes the relationship real. You can't fake it with God—He already knows. What He wants is for you to come to Him anyway, even when you're furious, even when you're ashamed, even when you're sure He's not listening.

Let me ask you this: do you think God would rather you get out your journal and take it out on Him, or go out on the streets and take it out on yourself instead? The answer isn't even close. God is strong—and He is your Father. God can take it.

If I Can, You Can.

Chapter 18:
Journaling

The ultimate measure of a man is not where he stands in moments of comfort and convenience, but where he stands at times of challenge and controversy.

-Martin Luther King Jr

One of the most underrated ways to stay mentally healthy? Journaling. Writing forces you to think; thoughts spark feelings, and feelings push you toward action—or sometimes hold you back. People often mistakenly assume that treatment is full of big daily breakthroughs, that you walk in and experience mindset shifts with every interaction or routine. Nope. It's the little habits, done over and over, that keep you steady.

Journaling is the same—a daily battle that takes time to win. Once you've made it a win, it stays with you until you choose to stop believing in its worth or stop prioritizing your mental health altogether. Ten years have passed since I stepped out of the facility, yet journaling is still just as essential as it was back then.

Why do so many people overlook it? Probably because anyone can do it. If you're over six, you can sit down and write. And honestly, some folks would rather tell their problems to anyone who'll listen. It's easier to spin a good sob story than to stare your truth in the face. I know—

because I did it. But you need one safe place where you can be brutally honest, no filters. For me, that place is my journal.

Why journal is the best place to dump your worries? Because no one interrupts you, no one rolls their eyes, and you don't have to prove your pain is worse than anyone else's. It's just you, a pen, and the truth. There's something raw about pouring your feelings out on paper—ugly, messy, unedited—and reading them later. It captures all your struggles and allow you to make sense of them. Sometimes I think, Wow, I can't believe I survived that. Other times, I realize I was stressed over nothing. That perspective alone is worth every second spent writing.

Whether I'm writing to God, venting about people, or jotting down a gratitude list, writing always delivers. And gratitude lists hit differently after getting off drugs and alcohol. One of my favorites? The fact that I didn't have to get my arm amputated after an infection from dirty needles. Every time I write, I'm grateful I can still use my left arm, I can't help but smile.

The day I walked out of treatment is still one of the happiest moments of my life. The rules and restrictions weren't mine to live by anymore. I could shower barefoot in my own bathroom. I could open the fridge when I wanted. I could decide my own bedtime without a lights-out call. Tiny freedoms I'd never noticed before suddenly felt like luxuries, worth fighting for.

Remembering those moments keeps me grateful and grounded. Gratitude isn't a cheesy exercise for me—it's deeply personal and hard-earned. Most of the time, it's just survival. And when we're finally beyond survival, it becomes the only thing that can truly help us grow, heal, and even break free of our most stubborn past patterns.

Not even grateful for the ones you've got? You might think you need to see blessings before you feel blessed, but that's a mind trick. No matter how rough life feels right now, there are millions who would trade places with you in a heartbeat. Never forget that—because it's true.

If I Can, You Can.

Chapter 19:
Physical Fitness

For I consider that the sufferings of this present time are not worth comparing with the glory that is to be revealed to us.

-Romans 8:18

All addicts have that *thing* in us. I don't really know how to describe it, but if you're reading this book you know exactly what I'm talking about. That *thing* needs an outlet and working out to me is the best way to keep it under control.

As I talked about a little bit earlier, in my addiction I got all the way down to 153lbs. When I got into rehab I ballooned up to almost 240lbs. One of the reasons I like to work out also is because it keeps my mind busy. Focusing on my physical health fills up those parts of my day when I would usually sit around and worry about life.

Want to talk about a high?

See how you feel after an intense workout. The stress relief alone is enough to make you never want to miss a day. To think that I went from 240lbs, abscess and track marks covering my arms to where I'm at today brings me nothing but a sense of pride and accomplishment. Watching what I eat and drinking a gallon of water each day are little things I do to remind myself to keep growing and never settle. Addicts always have to get better everyday. Growth is the name of the game.

I wasn't allowed to workout in rehab; it was strictly forbidden. But I knew I had to have it, so I would sneak into a warehouse bathroom every morning and do what we called "bathroom push-ups." Every single morning I would go and put my hands on that nasty, grimy floor. God knows what covered my hands when I put them on that bathroom floor, but I did not care one bit. Whatever the consequences, it was better than never waking up again after that short-lived high.

I had done so much damage to my body. I had starved my body for so long of vitamins, nutrients, and basic respect. So yes, I ate and ate and ate when I first got to treatment, but the more I looked into the mirror at 240 lbs, the more I knew it was time to put in the work to become healthy and strong. I knew I wanted to be the complete opposite of what I currently was, and getting in shape was a top priority, no excuses.

I learned a valuable lesson when I started working out. I was always trying to figure out what I could get from the gym. That was the wrong mindset for me. It's not about what I can get—it's about what I *can give*. The focus should remain on how much worry and pain I can shed while at it. If I can feel even one percent better about myself and my life after working out, that's worth the effort.

The best part of working out is there are so many avenues! Walking, dumbbells, boxing, yoga, pickleball, golf and the list goes on. The key is to find what you like and then make the workout intense. Mind, body & soul are the three components of a healthy life. The only thing better than looking good is feeling good and that's why we work out!

If I Can, You Can.

Chapter 20:
Reading

If you want others to value you, first, you have to value yourself.

-Unknown

Before treatment, you could have chased me around the block with a book. Why would I need to learn anything when I thought I already knew everything? There's an old saying that knowledge is power—but that's not entirely true. Applied knowledge is power. I once heard someone say that whatever you're going through, someone has already been through it—and there's a good chance they've written a book about it.

As an addict, my mind would race—and it still does at times. Reading helps calm it down. The key to turning your life around isn't just getting the drugs or alcohol physically out of your system. That's an important part, but recovery goes much deeper than detoxing. What truly changed my life for the better was—and always will be— growth. As addicts, we have to continually get better, smarter, and stronger. I didn't make the rules, but that's just how it is.

Just like writing, reading forces you to think. Once again, those thoughts take hold in your mind, and you get emotionally involved with them. Those emotions lead to action—or, in my case for so long, inaction.

There are books out there that will absolutely blow your mind. Psycho-Cybernetics by Dr. Maxwell Maltz teaches everything you need to know about self-image and the subconscious. Think & Grow Rich by Napoleon Hill showed me that whatever we constantly think about, we will bring into our reality. As a Man Thinketh by James Allen is another excellent read. All of these books continue to push youfurther and further into your destiny and have helped me almost as much as treatment did. And don't forget the ultimate guide: The Bible. There are so many incredible scriptures in there. I often wonder why preachers never talk about them—many are too busy trying to make you fear God rather than truly get to know Him.

As I mentioned earlier, reading was never my thing. I started with a goal of just 10 pages a day. Now, reading is a staple of my daily life. It took some time, but the rewards of gaining knowledge make it more than worth it.

If I Can, You Can.

Chapter 21:
Fight

If you are lonely when you're alone, you are in bad company.

-Jean-Paul Sart

By the time I went into treatment, I was exhausted. Even without the detox, I was just worn out. For the last eight years, I felt like I had been in a heavyweight boxing match, day in and day out. The physical and mental toll drugs had taken on me was undeniable. Add to that the fact that it took me almost two weeks to finally get some sleep after detox, and I was ready to give up. Whether I liked it or not, I had come to a fork in the road: I would either continue to fight myself or turn around and fight the real enemy.

I don't think it's a coincidence that the time I needed my energy the most was also the time I had the least. I was in the fight for my life. I was in the fight for my future. I was in the fight so I could one day tell my story—so my friends would not die in vain. Once I quit feeling sorry for myself, I decided to dig my heels in. I decided to get dirty. I decided that nothing would dare stop me from turning my life around. That's the type of energy I had to have. That's the type of focus that was required.

It required grit. If you feel like you've never had grit, try this: tighten your fist as hard as you can. That feeling—

the tightening of the muscles in your forearm—that's grit. That's the physical form of determination. To this day, when I feel my energy slipping, I just tighten my fist. In some strange way, it reminds me of what I overcame in my past.

Ever heard of David vs. Goliath? This was my Goliath. This was my once-in-a-lifetime chance to end the cycle of addiction that plagued both sides of my family for generations. Every single day in treatment, when I didn't want to get up, I got up. Every time I wanted to leave, I went and talked it through with someone. Every time I started to sweat before standing in front of the class to lay out the trauma from my past, I took a deep breath and said, "There is no going back, Sam."

In other words, I took that slingshot and rock and hit Goliath right in the middle of his big-ass forehead.

If I Can, You Can.

Chapter 22:
The End Aka The Beginning

The cave you fear to enter holds the treasure you seek.

-Joseph Campbell

The week I was leaving treatment, I experienced a wide range of emotions. I was ecstatic and terrified at the same time. I had grown comfortable in my safe space at treatment—which is exactly what it is and should be. My biggest fear was that five minutes after leaving the property, I would start thinking old thoughts and acting on them. And that's okay. It's okay to have those thoughts. I was being real and honest with myself. The key is not to stay in them. You've been preparing for this moment since the day you came into treatment. This is what it's all about: getting healthier and going out to live your life.

My friend, you deserve to live life to the fullest! You are God's highest form of creation. The capabilities already within your soul will shock you when you put them to the test. Stay connected and stay honest with the people you love. Smile. Enjoy the sunshine. Enjoy the small things in life that make it worth living. Will you have moments of weakness? Absolutely. I still do from time to time, but the difference now is that I know those moments are lies—and that is not who I am anymore!

What helped me the most was staying connected to

God, finding a job I enjoyed, staying close with healthy friends and family, and taking out any remaining anxiety in the gym. All of the habits I've discussed in this book—reading, journaling, and working out—are what keep me healthy. No question about it. I knew if I wanted to remain healthy, I had to take it into my own hands and handle my business. What will keep you winning in life are goals. The purpose of a goal is, of course, to achieve it—but it's the person you become in order to achieve those goals that really counts. That is where growth lies. And as we've discussed, the people who stop growing usually return to the same lifestyle. But we don't!

I'll say it one more time, and I mean it with every fiber of my being in my soul:

If I Can, You Can.

Epilogue

Do what you can, with what you have, where you are.

- Theodore Roosevelt

There is a moment that comes after the chaos and after the cheers. It is quiet. No counselor is watching the clock. No roommate is tossing in the next bed. No one is banging on your door telling you it is time for the group. It is just you, the mirror, and a simple question that refuses to leave: Who are you now?

I used to think recovery would hand me a new identity in a gift box. It did not. Recovery gave me tools, people, and a path. The identity had to be built. Brick by brick. Choice by choice. Five minutes at a time. Some mornings I still wake up with a knot in my stomach and a voice that says, Take the easy road. Old Sam knocks like a salesman who will not leave the porch. New Sam answers the door with truth, discipline, and prayer. Most days, that is enough.

If you are waiting for fear to disappear before you move, you will never move. The fear did not go away for me. I simply learned to carry it without letting it drive. I learned that my legs work even when my head is noisy. I learned that gratitude can cut through a rotten mood faster than any shortcut I ever chased. I learned that God does not do it for me. God does it through me when I show up and work.

Today, my life looks ordinary on purpose. I drink water. I make my bed. I train. I write. I read. I return calls. I show up for family. I forgive quicker. I apologize with changed behavior. I say no to people and places that pull me backward. I protect my peace like it is oxygen. When the day gets heavy, I reset the clock and win a small thing. A set of pushups. A page in the journal. A single call to someone who needs to hear my voice. Momentum is built in inches, not miles.

I still think about the funerals. Faces I loved. Hands I shook while my heart was numb. I think about parents who walked behind caskets that should have stayed empty. Survivor's remorse used to drown me. Now it points me. My friends do not get a second chance, so I live like I do. I honor them by staying honest, by staying free, by telling the truth when it would be more comfortable to hide. Pain became purpose because I refused to waste it.

If you are early on, you may think, I cannot hold this pace for a lifetime. You do not have to. Hold it for five minutes. Then stack another five. Boredom will visit. So will anger, pride, and the urge to fix everything in a single day. Remember Gene's line that saved many of us from bad decisions: if you want to quit, quit tomorrow. Give yourself one more sunrise before you throw away the ground you have gained. Most storms shrink after sleep.

There is a lie that says you must pick a perfect path. You do not. You need a faithful one. Pick a few non-negotiables and keep them. For me, it is God, the gym, the journal, and the book in my hand. Those four pillars hold up the house on ugly days. I do not debate them. I do them.

When life punches, I return to them, and the room inside my head gets bigger. Old fears fit in smaller corners when discipline grows.

I made amends slowly. Not with speeches. With rent paid on time. With calls returned. With birthdays attended sober, present, and early. With hard conversations that did not end in blame. With promises kept long after the rush of apology faded. The people I hurt did not owe me quick trust. I earned it with quiet consistency, the kind that stacks over seasons and turns doubt into peace.

Shame will try to rent space again. Let it pass. Speak the truth anyway. Tell the story you were certain you would never say out loud. Own your part without excuses. Do it in safe rooms with people who have earned the right to hear it. You are not weak for crying. You are not soft for asking for help. You are not broken beyond repair. You are a human being who learned the hard way and decided the learning would count.

Community saved me more than once. A text from a brother who saw the look in my eyes. A leader who sat with me in silence and did not try to fix me with slogans. A table where coffee and honesty had equal weight. When I drift, I put myself back in those rooms. I shake hands. I listen more than I talk. I leave with a plan, not just a feeling. Isolation is where the old life rehearses. Connection is where the new life practices.

To the families who never gave up, thank you. Boundaries felt like punishment when I was using. Now I see them as love with a backbone. To the men and women still bargaining with the old life, listen to me. There is nothing left out there for you. You have already tested every shortcut. Take the long road because it is the only road that truly gets you home.

I used to believe God was waiting to sentence me. Today I know He was waiting to walk with me. Some days I am loud with gratitude. Some days I am quiet and tired. Both days, He shows up when I do. Faith for me is not fireworks. Faith is laundry done, a call returned, a meeting sat through, a workout finished, a meal eaten that serves my body, and a bedtime honored, so tomorrow has a chance.

There will be seasons that press hard. Holidays that carry land mines. Anniversaries that smell like the worst day. Invitations that sound friendly and feel like a trap. Make a plan before the moment arrives. Bring your own car. Bring a brother or sister who knows your tells. Set a time to leave. Keep a number on your phone that you can call from the driveway. Freedom is not luck. Freedom is preparation repeated.

What comes next for you is not a mystery written in the stars. It is a pattern written in your calendar. Guard it. When you fall, fall forward. When you slip, tell on yourself fast and get back in the fight. When you win, celebrate without arrogance. Send that victory back into the world by helping someone else off the floor. The quickest way to keep your freedom is to give it away in service.

If you are reading this on a night that feels impossible, hear me. I have been on that floor. I have stared at the ceiling and thought, This is who I am now. It was not.

It is not. You can build again. You can love again. You can be trusted again. You can forgive the person in the mirror. You can become the person your family whispers prayers about when they think no one is listening.

I once counted down from ten with poison in my veins. Today I count up. One honest choice. Two hands steady on the wheel. Three deep breaths before I speak. Four pages in a book that sharpens my mind. Five minutes at a time. Six days stacked before a rest day, I have earned. Seven words whispered when the old voice returns: I do not live there anymore.

This is not a fairy tale. It is work. It is also joy that sneaks up on you in the most normal moments. A father's text. A mother's laugh. A quiet drive at sunset with no agenda except to get home safe. If that sounds small, you have not lived my old life. Small is sacred when you once lived only for the next high.

I learned to say no without writing an essay. No to the party that smells like yesterday. No to the favor that keeps me tied to a past I survived. No to the voice that says I owe people a version of me that almost died. Every no protects the yes that matters. Health. Family. Purpose. Sleep. A clear mind that can hear God when the world gets loud.

You made it to this page. That alone means something in you is ready. Do not waste that spark. Put it to work before it fades. Tell someone. Ask for help. Pick a pillar and start. Then stack five minutes on top of five minutes until a day has passed, and you can sleep with a clean conscience. Wake up and do it again. One day you will look up and realize you built a life out of simple choices that kept adding up.

I am not special. I am proof.

If I can, you can.

www.ingramcontent.com/pod-product-compliance
Lightning Source LLC
Chambersburg PA
CBHW071440300726
48976CB00004B/1400